Claiming Christmas

Claiming Series
Book 6

Violet Rae

Blurb

Snowed in together, can a Christmas miracle melt her doubts and lead them to a love meant for a lifetime?

Connor

When I took the position of deputy sheriff in the small town of Garland, Colorado, I just wanted to forget the horror I left behind in Houston, and fulfil the oath I took as an officer of the law to protect and serve. The last thing I expected was to find my perfect woman in the shape of beautiful sheriff's assistant, Jessica Monroe. Now all I need to do is convince her that she's all I want—not just for Christmas, but for life.

Jess

Connor Banks is kind, generous, and strong. He's also the most gorgeous man I've ever laid eyes on, but I know he'd never look twice at a woman like me—a woman with too many curves and a crippling lack of confidence due to my ex-boyfriend's cruel comments. But when the weather outside turns frightful, Connor and I find ourselves snowed in together at the station. With just our body heat to keep us warm, it's beginning to look a lot like … love.

Chapter 1
Jessica

I'm sitting at my desk, chewing idly on the end of my pen and staring blankly at my computer screen, when Sheriff Drayton Saunders walks back into the station.

"Call Jimmy at the garage and have him add chains to my tires," he says, making me jump as he drops his keys on my desk.

Drayton has only been in the job a few weeks, but he's done more for the small town of Garland in that time than the previous sheriff did in ten years. Ex-military, he was the perfect candidate to take over when Sheriff Bailey retired. He runs things firmly but fairly and has quickly earned the respect of colleagues and residents alike.

"Mine, too," Connor, the deputy, says, appearing around the corner with his keys in his hand. "I'm on call tonight., and I don't wanna get stuck in the snow. They're predicting quite a storm."

I sit up a little straighter in my chair. My heart rate picks up, thrumming against my ribs. Connor's presence does weird things to me—makes me shaky and hot despite the freezing temperatures outside.

Connor transferred here from Houston six months ago. I'm not sure why he'd want to give up the buzz of city life for our small town, but he's a great addition to our close-knit team here at Garland Sheriff's Office. He's handsome, hardworking, and damned good at his job. I'm pretty sure every red-blooded woman in town wants a piece of his nicely muscled ass.

Including me.

I'm ridiculously attracted to him, but there's no way I can tell him. What the hell could a small-town, mousy secretary have to offer a man who's used to the fast pace and excitement of the big city? I'm just your average curvy gal who lives alone with my cat, Dave. Plus, my ex-boyfriend robbed me of any self-confidence I may have had in the bedroom—which wasn't much to begin with.

"The storm is moving in sooner than they first thought. Looks as though it will hit us late tomorrow afternoon," I say, handing the sheriff a piece of paper with the weather report on it.

Drayton scans it over. "Put the word out that there's a weather curfew from 2 PM tomorrow. I want people in their homes where they'll be safe."

"You got it, boss." I nod.

I watch as the sheriff heads for his office, closing the door behind him. From the corner of my eye, I see Connor sauntering toward my desk, his eyes on the paper in his hands.

I look up at him with a bright smile as he comes to a halt in front of me. "Do you need something?"

He leans on the edge of my desk, and the action pulls his uniform pants tight across his muscular thighs. "Maybe you should stay home tomorrow," he suggests, his deep voice oozing through me like warm chocolate. "Most people will be leaving early anyway. A few of us are going to clear the snow and check the station is secure before the storm comes in."

"Thanks, but it's not like I live far. My apartment is above the bakery in town, so I'm within walking distance," I reply with a smile. "Besides, I have too much to do, ensuring everyone is prepared." I pause, chewing on the end of my pen again. "I guess I should get a tree from Snowflake Farm before the storm arrives."

"You like a real Christmas tree? Isn't it a little early?"

"Beginning of December is never too early," I argue. "Besides, these real trees last over a month if you take care of them. My apartment isn't big, so I always try to get a small tree. I love the smell of pine and camphor and citrus. I make these little gingerbread stars and hang them as decorations, and I have these cool rechargeable Christmas candles that look like the real deal. The "flame" flickers and everything. Oh, and the tree lights have about fifteen different settings—" I clamp my mouth shut, knowing I sound like a total Christmas geek.

Connor chuckles. "Big fan of Christmas, huh?"

"If it doesn't move, I decorate it." I laugh a little self-consciously.

"Want some company?"

I stare at him blankly. "Company?"

"This is my first Christmas in Garland. Most of my stuff is in storage back in Houston, so I need a tree and some decorations for my place. Makes sense to take my truck. I can get my tree and your smaller one on the roof rack."

My heart pounds at the thought of spending time with Connor outside work. Until now, our interactions have been purely professional—unlike my lascivious thoughts. "Um, yeah, that sounds good."

Connor nods. "We'll head to Snowflake Farm straight from work."

Excitement bubbles in my stomach, and I give him a beaming smile. "Okay. Good. Great." *Stop talking, Jessica!* "Well, I should call the garage to get those chains organized. I'm sure Jimmy is going to be inundated because of the storm. And I can't have you at risk out on patrol in these conditions."

"Not only do you keep me safe, but you also run this office practically single-handedly *and* make sure I have a fresh cup of coffee every morning. Is there anything you *can't* do?" Connor teases, his mouth tipping up in a smile that creates a dimple on his cheek that I want to lick.

"Oh, trust me, there's plenty I can't do. I can't cook for toffee, and I suck at abseiling."

His dark eyebrows pop up. "Abseiling?"

"Yeah. You know, where they put you in a harness, and you throw yourself down the side of a mountain on a rope. I volunteered to do it for charity last year and got stuck in a tree halfway down. I pushed off the rockface a little too enthusiastically," I say with a grimace. "I was dangling upside with a tree branch lodged up my . . . well, let's just say it was lodged where the sun don't shine for ten minutes before the guides got me untwisted."

Connor's mouth twitches and his blue eyes dance with amusement.

I glare at him. "It wasn't funny. You try hanging upside-down for ten minutes with these babies jammed in your face." I jab my generous boobs. "I nearly suffocated."

Connor's gaze drops to my chest. "They look mighty fine from here," he says softly.

His deep voice and the appreciation in his eyes send goosebumps skittering across my skin. "I think you need to get your eyes checked," I snort, getting the joke in first.

Connor frowns. "Why do you do that?"

I look at him blankly. "Do what?"

"Put yourself down."

I shrug. "I . . . guess I don't realize I'm doing it."

"You need to stop, Jessica. You're a beautiful woman. Any man would be lucky to have you."

I swallow hard. "I . . . You think I'm beautiful?"

"Beautiful, kind, intelligent." His blue eyes darken as they hold mine, and my breath gets stuck between my lungs and throat.

I can't look away. It's like he's staring into my soul. Like he sees me. *Really* sees me. Not the overweight woman with body image issues but the desirable woman who wants to melt into his sturdy, masculine frame.

Before I can formulate one of my usual witty comebacks, someone calls Connor's name, and he takes off to deal with their query.

Nervous perspiration prickles over my skin, and I stand and make my way to the ladies' room. I take a few deep breaths as I splash cold water on my hot cheeks. Grabbing some paper towels, I pat my face dry, staring at myself in the mirror. Hazel eyes gaze back at me from a rounded face in its frame of light-brown hair. Nothing exciting there unless you consider freckles sexy. My eyes slide down. Big boobs, thick thighs. I'm no one's idea of a femme fatale—as my ex-boyfriend liked to remind me regularly.

Yet here I am, twenty-four years old and practically swooning because a man told me I'm beautiful. And not just any man. Connor Sinclair—the man I've been secretly crushing on for months. But I can't go there, even if, by some miracle, he did reciprocate my feelings. I'm sure he was only being kind. After all, we work together. I'm the colleague who greets him with a mug of coffee every morning and tells him to be careful every time he goes out on patrol.

"Pull yourself together, Jessica," I tell my reflection.

Once I've composed myself, I head back to my desk and call the local garage, which promises to send someone over right away to add the snow chains to the sheriff's cruiser and Connor's truck. True to their word, they get them done in record time, and Connor heads out on patrol.

The day is busy and passes quickly, and I'm almost surprised when 5 PM rolls around. I head to the staff room and grab my purse and coat. Knowing it will be bitterly cold outside, I pull my woolly hat over my hair and grab my fleece-lined gloves.

Connor pokes his head around the staff room door and raises an eyebrow. "Ready to go tree hunting?"

I'm ready to go Connor hunting, but I keep that thought to myself and give him a beaming smile. "Let's do it."

Chapter 2
Connor

I'm not sure what possessed me to offer to go tree-shopping with Jessica —unless you count my unhealthy obsession with the gorgeous sheriff's assistant. The words were out of my mouth before my brain engaged, and the smile she gave me sent sparks of sunlight into my bloodstream.

I've spent the last six months trying not to notice her hazel eyes, cute freckles, and gorgeous curves. Her smile lights up the room, and her kindness and enthusiasm surround her like a warm glow. And she's incredibly good at her job, running the office with efficiency and confidence. Although, she seems to be sadly lacking that confidence on a personal level.

Jessica's reaction to my gentle flirting earlier was surprising. She seemed genuinely shocked to be complimented on her looks. Makes me wonder who's made her feel unworthy in that way. The thought stirs an unexpected pang of anger. The idea of anyone making Jessica feel less than the goddess she is doesn't sit well with me. At all.

"Warm enough?" I ask as Jessica sits next to me in the truck's passenger seat.

"It's toasty in here," she replies with her ever-present smile. "How was patrol?"

"Remarkably quiet, considering the forecast. It's one of the things I love about this town; the people listen and don't take stupid chances."

"Must be very different from policing in a big city," she observes.

I frown as dark memories slide over me. "You could say that."

"Sorry. I didn't mean to bring back bad memories."

I cast her a look, seeing her grimace. Instinctively, I reach for her hand, tucking it beneath mine on my thigh and giving her a reassuring smile. "You could never bring me bad memories, Jessica." I pause, choosing my words carefully. "Something happened in Houston. I don't talk about it."

Jessica squeezes my hand. "You don't need to talk about it. But for what it's worth, I'm sorry for whatever put that sadness in your eyes."

Her intuition surprises. She reads me so well, which is faintly unsettling.

Luckily, I'm saved from answering as we pull up at Snowflake Farm on the outskirts of Garland. I help Jessica from the truck, and we make our way to the rows of trees, our warm breath leaving plumes in the air.

We wander the rows, inspecting trees to find the right one. "What kind of tree do you want? Tall, small, thick?" Jessica asks.

"I need a big, manly tree," I tell her, straight-faced.

She snorts. "Manly?"

I nod. "Yeah. Big branches and a thick trunk."

She shakes her head as she laughs. "I'll make sure you get the manliest tree in the entire place."

Jessica turns right into a fenced-off area with more trees. I close the fence gate behind us, and she starts weaving among the trees with focused intent. "This is where they keep the best trees. The SEAL version," she says in a mock whisper like we're on some secret mission.

"And the most expensive, I assume?" I ask, my mouth twitching at her contagious enthusiasm.

Jessica shrugs. "You want a manly tree? This the place."

"Why don't you pick one for me?"

She cocks an eyebrow. "Really? You're trusting me to choose one with big enough branches and a thick trunk?"

Hearing those words spill from her lips causes a reaction south of my belt, and I'm suddenly glad for my bulky police-issue jacket.

I clear my throat. "I trust you, Jessica."

Her hazel eyes kindle, and her smile widens. She pulls her coat closer around her body and strolls through the pines. I watch as she trails her hands through their leaves, pausing periodically to rub the needles between her fingers and lean in to inhale their scent.

"Seems like a shame to cut these down," she murmurs. Then her gaze is captured by the next tree, which reaches into the night sky, with full, broad branches. "This one. This is your tree," she says, turning to face me.

I nod. "This one it is."

I find a staff member, and we step back to let him do his thing. He chops the tree down with efficient ease, and it hits the ground with a thud.

Jessica chooses a smaller tree with fluffy branches, and with the staff member's help, we get them back to the truck and strapped down.

Next, we head into the Christmas store attached to the tree farm, immediately assaulted by an array of sparkling lights, glittering decorations, and upbeat Christmas music.

Jessica looks like a kid in a candy shop as she takes everything in.

"Something tells me I'm going to lose you in here." I chuckle.

"Isn't it amazing?" she asks, her hazel eyes sparkling.

"That's one word for it," I say softly. My eyes drink in her flushed cheeks from our short walk from the parking lot before landing on hers.

Heat sizzles between us, and the lights and music fall away, leaving us suspended in a private moment. Jessica's eyes kindle with some deep emotion that steals my breath. She affects me as no woman ever has, endangering my wary heart.

A staff member makes an announcement over the tannoy, breaking the spell, and Jessica blinks as if surfacing from a dream.

"So, um, what kind of decorations do you need?" she asks, a slight wobble to her voice.

"Uh, everything," I reply with a sheepish look.

Jessica gets that look again, the same one she had when choosing my tree. I almost expect her to roll up her sleeves and wait for the starting pistol. God, she's adorable. Irresistible. Perfect for me.

We wander aisle after aisle until my eyes swim with white spots from the glare of all the decorations. Jessica tells me I need a theme for my tree, and I'm happy to stand back and let her choose a color scheme. At this point, I'm more fascinated with her than what kind of baubles are going on my new tree. She outshines all of the festive glitz in this store.

We settle on buying white lights, silver glass balls, and wooden ornaments, which will add a rustic look to the tree. As we trek around the store, she starts slipping her hand into mine unless she's sorting through ornaments and lights. It seems so natural, and I don't think she even realizes she's doing it, but each time she slides her smaller hand into mine, a warm buzz extends up my arm. It's such a sweet, simple gesture, but it has my heart clenching and lava bubbling in my loins.

Jessica grabs some decorations for herself, and once we've paid at the checkout, we head back to the truck. She walks toward the arch that leads to the parking lot but stops suddenly and looks up. I follow her gaze.

"Mistletoe," she whispers. "We can't violate the laws of Christmas, or we'll have bad luck for the entire year."

I glance at the innocent-looking berries wrapped in red ribbon and wonder if fate is giving me a nudge.

Surprising us both, I stride toward her and pull her against me, the bags of decorations forgotten on the ground. "As deputy sheriff, it's my duty to uphold the laws of Christmas."

I cup her face in my hands and brush my lips against hers, a fleeting contact that doesn't come close to satisfying my needs.

"Think that was enough to uphold the law?" she whispers, her eyes soft on my face.

I groan. "Not even close."

I gather Jessica closer so her body is flush against mine and claim her lips the way I've longed to since I first laid eyes on her. I indulge myself, drowning in her taste, the sensation of her soft lips, and how she fits in my arms. She melts into me, and her mouth opens eagerly, meeting my kiss with equal passion. I sweep my tongue over her lips, needing more of her addictive taste. I nip at her bottom lip, and she gasps. I take advantage and slide my tongue inside to meet hers.

Her soft moan sets me on fire, and she winds her arms around my neck. My hands find her hips, pressing her delicious curves even more tightly to my hardness.

Reality returns with a vengeance at the blare of a car horn.

I pull back, trying to catch my breath and regain control. "I'm sorry, I—"

Jessica's fingers press against my mouth, stalling my words. "Don't apologize for the best kiss of my life."

I drink in her sparkling eyes and flushed cheeks.

Yeah, I'm in trouble.

Chapter 3
Jessica

My lips still tingle as Connor helps me into the truck and places our bags in the back. My cheeks flush hot as I remember how I tempted him to kiss me. I've never been one to initiate intimacy, mainly since my one and only boyfriend made me so conscious of my size. I loved my curves before Paul, who constantly remarked about my wide hips, chunky thighs, and the little fat roll on my stomach. Apparently, these things made me less desirable in his eyes, and I hate that I allowed him to steal my confidence.

But if the way Connor kissed me beneath the mistletoe is anything to go by, he loves my curves. The way he pulled me close and held me, his hands gripping my hips as he ravished my mouth . . .

I release a shaky breath, trying to gather my scattered wits as Connor drives into town, pulling up in the small parking lot at the rear of a rank of shops. My apartment is above the bakery and is accessed by a flight of external stairs.

Connor unstraps my tree from the truck and carries it up the stairs while I unlock the door. He props the small tree against the wall while I grab the tree stand with its built-in reservoir, and between us, we get it secured.

I stand back to look at my small, bare tree before switching my gaze to Connor. "Wanna help me decorate my tree in exchange for food?"

Connor quirks an eyebrow, and his intense blue gaze does odd things to my heart rate as it roves over my body. "Depends what's on the menu."

I lick my lips and clear my throat. I'd very much like to be on the menu for this man, but . . . "Um, I have beef stew and dumplings in the crockpot."

Connor closes his eyes and lets out a groan that sends goosebumps chasing up my arms. "My favorite. My mom used to make that when I was a kid."

I beam at him as I tug off my hat, gloves, and coat, hanging them up before taking Connor's heavy jacket and doing the same. Crossing to the large dresser, I open one of the base doors and pull the box of Christmas lights from the back, handing them to Connor.

"Can you do the lights while I sort the decorations?"

He gives me a suspicious look. "Is this the part where I have to find the one dodgy bulb that controls all the others before the lights will work?"

"Um, no?" I say hopefully.

Connor plugs in the bundle of lights. "Well, what do you know? They all work."

I unpack the ornaments and lay them out for easy access while Connor wraps the lights around the tree.

Decorating with Connor is fun, and we work in companionable silence. He looks strangely at home in my small apartment, and my heart sighs at the sight of him hanging trinkets on the branches. He's big, brawny, and handsome with his ocean-blue eyes, high cheekbones, and strong jaw. He's a private person, and although he's polite to everyone he works with, I have a feeling I'm seeing a softer side of him that he doesn't share with others.

Even though we haven't spoken about it, our kiss under the mistletoe replays in my mind. The way he held me, the clench of his hands on my hips, his mouth firm and demanding on mine. I could have kissed him for hours. Days. I crave him in a way I've never experienced before, not just physically but on every level. I want to soothe the pain in his eyes when he thinks no one is looking and see them crinkle with happiness instead.

It doesn't take long to get the job done, mainly because the tree isn't large. The finished product is a mix of old and new decorations, and the tree glows in pretty shades of red and gold.

Then we eat. We settle on the sofa with *It's a Wonderful Life* in the background on Netflix as Connor demolishes the massive helping of stew I dished up for him.

Once his bowl is empty, he leans back and rubs his stomach with a groan of satisfaction that rumbles from his chest. "That was delicious, thank you. You're an amazing cook."

Warmth blooms in my stomach at his compliment. "Believe me, there's no cooking involved," I say, finishing my last mouthful. "I chuck all the ingredients into the crockpot in the morning, and it's done when I get home. Cooking isn't my thing," I admit wryly. "Now baking, that's another thing altogether. My grandma taught me all her best recipes when I was growing up. I still have her recipe book held together with tape and a prayer."

Connor's blue eyes capture mine. "You were close with your grandma?"

I smile wistfully. "Yeah. She was . . . everything."

Connor reaches for my hand, linking his fingers with mine and smoothing his thumb over my skin. "I'm sorry."

I shake my head. "Don't be. All my memories of her are happy ones. I don't remember my grandpa. He and Grandma moved here from England after they got married. Grandpa died when I was little, and Grandma pretty much raised me."

Connor frowns and opens his mouth to ask a question when a ball of ginger fur jumps onto my lap.

"Dave! Where've you been, sweetie?" I coo, scratching behind his ears. "Were you sleeping on the bed?"

Dave bunts me under the chin, purring loudly.

"You named your cat Dave?" Connor asks, his mouth twitching.

I glare at him. "What? I happen to like the name. We don't all have to name our cats Tiddles or Fluffykins."

He laughs, the sound rich and deep. "You're adorable."

My breath hitches as his big, warm hand moves to cup my face, and I lose myself in his swirling eyes. I lean toward him involuntarily, my eyes dropping to his mouth, wanting his kiss more than my next breath. Closer . . . closer until . . . Dave pops his furry head up between us and licks Connor's chin.

A giggle breaks free as Dave rubs himself against Connor, purring loudly. "You're honored. He's not a fan of strangers, but he likes you."

Connor grins, and it changes his face, making him look younger and more carefree. "Seems I have the Dave seal of approval."

I blow out a shaky breath, deciding to go for broke. "You have the Jessica seal of approval, too."

Connor's eyes hold mine for a long moment, heat simmering in their depths. Then the sadness returns, and the shutters come down.

"I should go. Busy day tomorrow," he says abruptly, dislodging Dave as he surges to his feet.

My stomach drops to my feet. "I . . . okay."

"Thanks for the meal, Jessica," he says, grabbing his jacket. "I'll see you tomorrow. At work."

"At work. Right," I whisper. It's like he's reminding me of our relationship. Professional. Deputy sheriff and sheriff's assistant. Nothing more. Hot kisses notwithstanding.

As I close the door behind him, I realize that the best evening of my life didn't mean the same to him.

***

I arrive at work the following morning after a restless night with the beginnings of a headache throbbing behind my eyes. I press the pads of my fingers against my temples and sigh, knowing it's going to be a long day. I need coffee.

Connor is notable by his absence, and I can only assume he's on patrol preparing for the coming storm. I couldn't settle after he left last night and distracted myself by making enough ginger star biscuits to decorate three Christmas trees. I boxed up a dozen tied with a ribbon, intending to give them to Connor as a small Christmas gift.

The day passes quickly. I love my job, and the variety keeps my brain busy. Providing administrative support is only the tip of the iceberg—I screen visitors and telephone calls, deal with complaints, manage projects, act as staff support to the Sheriff's Parole Board, liaise between the sheriff and senior sworn officers, handle gun permit requests, and schedule appointments for the sheriff, deputy, and senior staff.

The phones are particularly busy today due to the incoming bad weather and queries from concerned residents. I call the local radio station and ask them to make an announcement advising the residents to head home before the snowstorm hits town. This storm is going to unleash a ton of snow, so it's better to cover all avenues to ensure peoples' safety.

I finish the call as Drayton appears beside me, and I fill him in on my progress.

"Why don't you head on home before it gets bad," he says, glancing at the report I've just finished typing up for him. "Don't want my favorite assistant at risk in this weather."

"Your *only* assistant," I scoff, touched by his concern.

"Couldn't do what I do without you, Jessica," he tells me with a rare smile.

Drayton Saunders is a serious man and doesn't dish out compliments readily, which makes his praise all the more special.

Rumor has it he was shipped home after being caught in a bomb blast in Helmand, but he doesn't speak about it. I know his father, Danny, who owns The Hideaway—the only bar in town—is incredibly proud of his son. If anyone can take care of themselves in this job, it's Drayton Saunders. Years in the military prepared him for any emergency.

"I, uh, think I'll stay here tonight if it's okay with you. Be good for Connor to have an extra pair of hands on the phones in case it gets busy," I'm surprised to hear the words spilling from my mouth, and warmth hits my cheeks at Drayton's knowing smile.

I hadn't planned to stay. My brain seems to have momentarily disengaged from my mouth. Somehow, I've just volunteered to spend the night at the station. With Connor. Just the two of us.

If the sheriff suspects anything, he doesn't say and nods in agreement. "Good idea, so long as you're sure."

"Dave uses a litter tray, and his food releases on a timer, so he should be fine on his own."

Drayton gives me a strange look. "Is Dave your boyfriend?"

"What? No! My cat."

"Thank God," he says, shaking his head. "You had me worried there for a minute." He pauses. "You called your cat Dave?"

"What is it with everyone questioning my cat's name? Yes, he's called Dave. It's a good, strong name for a ginger tom."

Drayton doesn't reply, instead glancing at the clock on the wall, which shows a little after noon. "I won't be back unless you need me. Connor should be on his way back now. I'm going to patrol around town to make sure everyone is shutting up shop and heading home."

"Okay, boss. You be careful out there," I say with a worried frown.

He lifts a hand in farewell. "Always."

Chapter 4
Connor

Once the chains are on the tires, I drive through town, putting out hazard signs where the roads become treacherous in the snow and ice. Not that anyone should be on the streets after 2 PM, but it's better to be safe than sorry. We've already had some snow, but it's nothing compared to what's forecast to hit in a few hours.

As I patrol, I see people hurrying home, storeowners closing up, and porches and walkways being cleared and salted. Drayton will do another patrol in a few hours, but for now, I'm satisfied that the residents are taking this storm warning seriously.

Thick flakes are beginning to swirl through the air as I head back to the station and park the truck in the lot. Just as I'm about to climb out, my phone lights up, and I smile when I see who the caller is.

I hit the answer button and put the phone to my ear. "Hey, kiddo."

"Ugh! You know I hate it when you call me that," Rosie huffs.

My baby sister is a sweetheart. I miss her like crazy since I left Houston for this small town in Colorado. I miss her big smile and her even bigger heart. Rosie is like a little ray of sunshine, spreading happiness and light wherever she goes.

Her sunny disposition makes her susceptible to the predators of this world, and guilt forms a fist in my gut because I'm not there to look out for her—something I've been doing since the day she was born. My mom remarried after my father's death, and Rosie was the product of that union. I was fifteen when she came into the world, and I've always taken my responsibilities as big brother seriously.

"Are you coming home for Christmas?" she demands, getting straight to the point.

I sigh. I knew this conversation was coming. "I don't think so, honey. Too many memories."

"Memories are portable, Con. You take them with you," Rosie points out. "Plus, it wasn't your fault. There was nothing you could've done."

I'm pretty sure my baby sister has been here before because she has the wisdom of a much older soul.

"I know. It wasn't just that. It was the whole set-up, Rosie. The politics and paperwork. I became a police officer to help people and keep people safe. Not to sit behind a desk pushing a pen. Garland is small, but I feel like I'm doing some good here, you know? The new sheriff is great, and he's turning things around, making some positive changes."

Rosie sighs down the line. "You're talking like you're never coming back."

Garland was only supposed to be temporary—a chance to get my head on straight again after what happened in Houston, but the longer I'm here, the more I find to like about the place.

In particular, the curvy temptress who brings me coffee with a gorgeous smile every morning. I look forward to that smile, to those wide hazel eyes, and that cute nose with its smattering of freckles. Jessica Monroe is my perfect woman—and she hasn't got a fucking clue.

She doesn't know I gape at her like a lovesick teenager when she's engrossed in her work. She doesn't know that I check to ensure she gets home safely when she works late. And she certainly doesn't know about my hard-as-fuck dick whenever I'm within touching distance of her.

It's been years since my cock paid attention to a woman, but now that he has, he's like a sniffer dog intent on claiming the Class A drug between her legs. And I'm confident that her pussy is every bit as addictive as I've imagined when I rub my cock raw to the image of her every night.

"Connor?" Rosie prompts, pulling me from my thoughts.

"Sorry, kiddo. Been a long day already. The whole town is getting ready for a big snowstorm."

"Oh, I bet it's beautiful there at Christmastime. I can just picture the snow and the twinkling lights and drinking hot cocoa in front of an open fire after a snowball fight," she sighs whimsically.

"Sorry to burst your bubble, but it's more like dangerously icy roads, frozen water pipes, and frostbite," I chuckle.

"I prefer my version," she laughs, ever the optimist. "You know, if you're not coming here for the holidays, maybe I'll just have to come to Garland."

"Like Mom and Sam would let you spend Christmas anywhere but with them," I scoff, knowing it would break their hearts.

"Well...we can all come," she says quickly.

Rosie has a solution for everything.

"If this snow keeps coming, you'll need a snowplow to get through," I say.

"How about a fire engine? I could always ask Dex. I'm sure he'd let me borrow one," Rosie says as if she's seriously considering it.

My eyes narrow. "Dex?"

"He's a firefighter. It's early days, but...I really like him," she admits.

"Since when are you old enough to date?" I grumble.

"I'm twenty-two, Connor, not twelve," Rosie laughs.

"So, this Dex. How old is he? Where does he live? What are his intentions?"

"Thirty-one. Sugar Land. And as for his intentions, that's between him and me," Rosie says firmly. "If you come back for Christmas, you can meet him," she says hopefully.

I chuckle. "Nice try. So long as he knows you have an older brother who will hand him his ass if he does anything to hurt you, we'll get along just fine."

"He's special, Connor. He likes me just the way I am. He doesn't seem to notice my size," Rosie says softly.

"Why do you women do that?" I ask with a frown. "Not all men like skinny women. Some of us like something to hold onto."

"Yeah, Dex is making me realize that," she sighs.

"How's it going at the Lockhart Club? Has the owner realized what a genius you are and promoted you yet?" I ask.

Rosie chuckles. "Jensen is great. The club was having some financial difficulties, so Jensen went to a financial consultancy for help. For a minute there, I thought I was going to be looking for another job, but they sent Poppy, and she's turned things around here."

"You'll always get work, honey. You're good at what you do, and you have that degree in hospitality management to fall back on," I say proudly.

"Yeah, but I like it at the Lockhart Club. The people are great, and Jensen pays well."

"Then make sure he knows what he'd be missing if you left," I advise. "Listen, kiddo. I gotta get going. Still lots to do before this storm hits."

"Okay. Love you, Con."

"Love you, too, kiddo."

I end the call and pocket my phone, feeling guilty again at the sadness in my sister's voice.

As I walk toward the station entrance, I see my colleagues shoveling snow from the walking paths. Shoving my keys into my coat pocket, I grab one of the shovels and get stuck in.

The snow isn't too deep, so it doesn't take long, but the temperature is dropping rapidly, and my hands are already numb despite my fleece-lined gloves. By the time we've shielded the windows and secured the outside of the station, we're all chilled to the bone. We traipse inside to find hot drinks waiting for us, courtesy of the one woman I can't seem to stop thinking about.

Jessica.

Five feet seven of delectable curves and eyes like warm molasses.

I stand in the corner, cradling my mug of coffee between my hands, wishing it was Jessica's face I was cradling while I kiss her senseless again. My eyes follow her helplessly as she moves around the room. Her whole face is alight as she smiles and hands out hot drinks. She doesn't know it, but just looking at her gets me hard. She's everything I've ever wanted in a woman, with her silky chestnut hair, plump lips, and sunny personality. She's fucking adorable. Too good for a man like me. I've got a good ten years and a shitload of baggage on her.

Even if the attraction were mutual, it's never a good idea to mix business with pleasure.

I watch as Jessica walks over to Officer Shaw and hands him the last of the steaming mugs. She turns to leave, but Shaw wraps his hand around her arm and says something that makes her laugh.

Anger claws up my throat. Shaw is a good guy, but I have the sudden urge to rip his arm off, the one that's touching Jessica. I grind my teeth together, trying to calm down. How close are they? I've never seen Jessica show any interest in him, but that doesn't mean she's not attracted to him. I don't want another man touching her.

She's mine.

My feet are already moving toward her as the thought pops into my head, but I pull up short when Adeline, the only female officer at the station, appears in front of me.

She's an attractive woman in her late twenties, tall, blonde, and slim.

"Hey, Connor," she says with a cheery smile. "I was wondering, since we're done for the day, if you'd like to come over to my place for dinner. I have hot soup and fresh bread. We can throw a blanket on the floor, have an indoor picnic, and hunker down together until the storm passes. What do you think?" she asks, giving me her most seductive smile.

It leaves me cold. Adeline leaves me cold.

She's been flirting and dropping less-than-subtle hints that she's available and willing for weeks. I've tried to keep my distance, not make a big deal of it, but she's turned up the heat in the last few days, and I'm done humoring her.

"Sorry, Adeline, but I'm on call tonight. I'll be at the station all night."

"Oh! Well, then, maybe I can keep you company?" she suggests, placing her hand on my forearm.

I curse myself for having walked straight into that one, and I'm trying to formulate a suitable reply when Jessica appears behind Adeline.

"Sorry, Adeline, but Drayton has already signed off on my overtime to stay and help Connor tonight," she tells Adeline with a bright smile.

I stare at Jessica in shock, but her attention is on the other woman. Is she telling the truth, or is she bailing me out of an awkward situation with Adeline? I'm hoping it's both.

"In that case, I'll stay, too. More hands at the pumps, so to speak," Adeline says, giving Jessica a saccharine-sweet smile.

"Afraid not," Jessica says, shaking her head sadly. "Drayton doesn't want anyone else in the building. Health and safety, or something."

Adeline's mouth tightens. "I see." She deliberately turns her back on Jessica. "My offer of dinner stands once the storm has passed."

"Thanks, but I'll pass," I reply with a tight smile.

"I see," Adeline says again. She gives Jessica a final glare before turning on her heel and stomping off.

"Well, that wasn't at all awkward," I say with a grimace. "Thanks for stepping in," I add, turning my gaze to Jessica.

She smiles. "You looked like a squirrel caught in headlights."

"Deer."

"Huh?"

I chuckle. "It's a deer caught in headlights."

Jessica laughs, and the husky sound shoots straight to my dick.

"Deer. Squirrel. Adeline. All the same," she says with a cheeky wink. "It's hard to turn down a woman without looking like a complete cockwomble."

I burst out laughing. "Cockwomble?"

"Isn't it a great word? It's British slang for an obnoxious person," she says enthusiastically.

"Right. Well, thanks for saving me from being a... cockwomble," I grin. Jessica has a way of making me forget my troubles. When I'm with her, I feel...peaceful. "So, did you mean what you said? About staying here tonight?"

"Yeah. I thought I could help on the phones or, you know, whatever," she says. "You okay with that?"

I capture her warm brown gaze with mine. "More than okay, Jess. I can't think of anyone else I'd rather spend the night with."

"Right. Good. Okay, then. I'll, um, I'll see you later." She lifts a hand in an awkward wave, her cheeks flushed with color.

I catch hold of her hand before she can move away. The sensation of her soft skin against mine has my balls tightening behind my zipper. "Just to be clear, if that had been you earlier, offering me soup and an indoor picnic, my answer would've been a resounding yes."

"I, uh—"

"Connor, can you come take a look at this before I leave?" Officer Shaw asks, holding up a report.

Jessica slips away, almost tripping over her feet in the process, and I smile. Yeah, she's feeling the same things I am. We're going to be the only two people in the station tonight, and I'm not sure how I'm going to keep my hands off her.

The temperatures outside may be dropping rapidly, but the heat inside is ramping up to melting point.

Chapter 5
Jessica

The wind is picking up. I can hear it howling outside and rattling the windows. Everyone else has gone home, so it's just Connor and me in the building—or it was until an hour ago when he got a call out. Apart from that, the phones have been quiet—just a few calls from elderly residents seeking the reassurance of a human voice.

Did Connor mean what he said earlier? About saying yes if I was the one asking him for a date? It's the second time he's flustered me with his words today. Not to mention his touch. When he held my hand in his, my nerve endings lit up like a thousand twinkling Christmas lights.

Goosebumps break out on my skin, and I shiver. Before I can second guess myself, I head for the storeroom, grabbing an armful of blankets. Then I take the seat cushions from the chairs in the reception area and place them on the floor, covering them with the blankets to make a cozy seating area.

I make some tuna sandwiches in the small kitchen and put them on a plate with potato chips and pickles. Then I make a flask of coffee, knowing Connor will appreciate something warm when he gets back, and carry everything back through to the office, laying it all out next to the blankets.

I bite my lip uncertainly. I could be committing professional suicide doing this, but it feels like Connor and I have been dancing around each other for months. My confidence took a hit, courtesy of my ex, but I can't let that stop me from taking a chance on someone else. On Connor. And if it turns out I've misread the situation, I guess I'll have to move to the mountains of Kathmandu and spend the rest of my life milking mountain goats.

Before I can overthink things any further, the door opens, and I look up to see Connor brushing snow from his police-issue jacket.

"Everything okay?" I ask.

"All good. Will Parker slid off the road and got his back tires stuck in the snow."

"Oh, no! Is he hurt?"

"Not a scratch. He was driving slowly, so there was no damage to him or the car. We managed to get the tires dug out between the two of us, and I followed him home," he says, running a hand through his damp hair.

My eyes cling to his tall frame. He's mouthwateringly attractive with his piercing blue eyes and olive-toned skin.

"Let's hope that's the worst thing that happens tonight," I say hopefully.

"I'm sure everything will be fine. It's like a ghost town out there. Everyone is tucked up safely in their homes and—" He trails off as he moves closer and his eyes fall on my little makeshift seating area.

I lick my lips nervously. "I was, uh, hoping you'd join me for that indoor picnic we talked about earlier. I know you're on call, but you still need to eat, so I've made sandwiches, and we have potato chips and pickles. I'm sure you must be cold, so there's a flask of coffee to warm you up if—"

Connor reaches me in three long strides, and the next thing I know, I'm wrapped up in his arms with his mouth on mine. He licks across the seam of my mouth, and I open up for him with a whimper, meeting the thrust of his tongue with my own. His scent and taste envelop me, woodsy and earthy, scattering every one of my senses to the howling wind outside.

His kiss is everything I dreamed of and more. Intoxicating. Addictive. Devastating.

My breasts flatten against his hard chest, and a sound rumbles up from his throat, something between a groan and a growl. The sound vibrates through me and across my sensitized skin, tightening my nipples.

We're both gasping for breath when he finally breaks the kiss, dropping his forehead to mine.

"Holy crap," I whisper.

He smiles. "Yeah. Been wanting to kiss you for months."

I pull back to look at him. "Why didn't you?"

He shrugs. "Too old for you. Too much baggage."

I shake my head, smoothing a hand across his cheek. "Why don't you let me be the judge of that?"

Connor turns his head, placing a kiss on my palm. "You don't have a judgmental bone in your body, Jess, and that's the problem. You're kind and generous. You light up a room when you smile. It's one of the first things I noticed about you. That and these goddamn sexy curves," he says, cupping my ass.

I laugh bitterly. "My ex didn't think they were sexy."

"Fucking idiot." Connor glowers. "Wanna tell me about it over a coffee and pickles?" he asks, tipping his head toward the blankets.

Warmth spreads through my chest as he links his fingers with mine and tugs with him. He pours us a coffee from the flask, handing me my mug as I settle myself cross-legged on the blankets. I watch as he sinks down next to me, admiring how his uniform shirt molds his wide chest and firm biceps. I gulp my hot coffee, yelping as I almost give my tongue third-degree burns.

Jesus, Monroe, could you be any less sexy?

This man has got me so off-balance, I don't know my curvy ass from my elbow.

"So, how long were you with this ex and did he have a visual impairment?" Connor asks with a frown.

"A year, and no."

"A personality impairment, then," Connor states.

My mouth turns up in a reluctant smile. "That, and a wayward penis."

Connor almost chokes on his coffee. "Wayward penis?"

"Yeah. It kept finding its way inside the local barmaid," I say wryly.

"The barmaid that Danny fired for stealing?" Connor asks, referring to Drayton's father, who owns the only bar in town.

I nod. "The same."

"Sounds to me like you had a lucky escape," he observes.

"I realize that, with hindsight. But he did a lot of damage to my self-esteem. I've always been self-conscious about my size, and he knew which buttons to press, telling me how lucky I was to have a man like him who could overlook my extra rolls and my weight. He even told me once that he used to imagine I was someone else when we had sex."

"Asshole," Connor growls, his blue eyes darkening with anger. "Men who stoop to that level are bullies trying to compensate for their own... *shortcomings*," he says meaningfully.

"If you're suggesting he had a small cock, you'd be right," I say bluntly. "I feel like such an idiot now, allowing someone to treat me that way. I know I'm overweight, but my size doesn't define who I am."

"Jess, you're gorgeous. I haven't been able to take my eyes off you since the day I walked through that door and saw you sitting at your desk, sucking on the end of your pen. It's weird being jealous of a goddamned pen."

My eyes widen. For once, I'm speechless, shocked by Connor's admission. "I—"

"I told myself I was too old for you, too fucked-up by what happened in Houston. But the truth is, when I close my eyes and picture my perfect woman, I picture you, Jess."

I don't know what to say. I'm his perfect woman? I've never been anyone's perfect anything. Part of me wants to throw myself into his arms and beg him to make love to me, while another part wants to ease the pain I can see in his eyes.

"Will you tell me what happened?" I ask softly.

Connor is silent for so long, I'm about to apologize for pressing him to share when he starts talking.

"I was about to go off duty when the call came in. A hit and run involving a young woman. Paramedics were on their way, but I was only a few blocks away, so I hit the blues. I was first on the scene, and..." he stops abruptly, and his throat works as he swallows hard.

Without thinking, I move close, wrapping my arms around him. He holds himself rigid for a few seconds before his arms come around me, and he hugs me back. I rest my head in the crook of his neck, silently offering him my strength as he fights to gain control of his emotions.

"The woman was in her mid-twenties. The driver had hit her on a crosswalk and tossed her body a hundred yards down the street. She was six months pregnant."

"Oh, shit," I whisper, closing my eyes on a wave of emotion.

"There was nothing I could do. I just held her in my

arms while she died. The paramedics tried to resuscitate her, but she was gone."

Connor stops again, his chest heaving as he sucks in a breath. I squeeze him a little tighter as if I can hold him together while he relives the horror of that day.

"Did they get the guy?" I ask when Connor remains silent.

He nods. "Yeah, they got him. He was three times over the limit. I testified in court, but all he got was a hefty fine and a suspended sentence."

I pull back to look at him in shock. "*What?* But... he took a life! *Two* lives," I say, swallowing hard as I think about that poor woman and her baby. Was she married? What about the baby's father? What the hell must he be going through? "How can anyone get away with that?" I ask, trying to wrap my head around it and failing.

"He's the son of a senator. That should tell you everything you need to know," Connor says bitterly. "Money, power, and reputation matter more than two innocent lives. I joined the force to do good, not watch criminals go free because daddy made it all disappear. That's not justice."

"So you asked to be transferred here?"

Connor smiles wryly. "Not exactly. I was put on administrative duties and offered therapy. But the whole experience made me question everything. I took an oath when I joined the force. How the fuck could I sit at a desk pushing papers around when a pregnant woman died in my arms, and the man who did it was still walking around a free man?"

"It wasn't your fault, Connor," I whisper, tilting my head to look up at him. The pain in his eyes makes my chest ache and has the tears I've been holding in spilling down my cheeks. "You did everything you could. At least she wasn't alone when she died. You gave her comfort in her last moments."

Connor frowns as if he hasn't considered that. "I couldn't face going back out on the streets. I went on a downward spiral for a few months. Started drinking too much and not sleeping enough. My captain eventually took me to one side, told me his cousin was the sheriff here, and the position of deputy had come up. He didn't give me much choice, said I either transferred here for six months, or he'd declare me unfit for duty."

My stomach drops. "For six months? But you've already been here that long. Does... does that mean you're leaving?"

Connor shakes his head, weaving his fingers through my hair and tilting my head back. "No. Turns out my captain did me a huge favor. He's a good man. I think he knew coming to Garland would be good for me. I've become fond of this little town and the people in it. And one of the people in it has managed to worm her way under my defenses and into my heart," he says, his intense blue gaze holding mine.

My heart stops. Literally stops for an entire beat. When it picks up again, it feels like it's going to beat its way out of my chest and into Connor's to find its mate.

I search his eyes. "I don't understand. Why would you want someone like me instead of the Adeline's of this world?"

Connor's mouth tightens in anger. "I could strangle your ex-asshole for ever making you doubt yourself, Jess. For not seeing you the way I see you. Because when I look at you, I see a woman with a beautiful soul and a gorgeous body I want to lose myself in. The second I kissed you, you were mine. And I'll never leave you in any doubt about how sexy you are. How fucking hard you make me. You'll never doubt how much I want you, in and out of the bedroom. Grief brought me to Garland, but you've given me a reason to stay. If you'll have me."

Chapter 6

Connor

"I'll have you any way you like, Connor Banks," Jess says, her molten brown gaze melting my insides and hardening my cock. "Rolled in eggs and flour, dipped in melted chocolate, smothered in cinnamon butter and—"

I cut her off, kissing her hard and then nipping at her bottom lip. "Do you have some kind of food fetish?"

"I'm not sure yet. Can I let you know?" she asks breathlessly, threading her hands through my hair and tugging my head back down to hers.

I chuckle as our mouths meet, slow and sweet this time. But then Jess grinds herself against me with a needy moan, and my willpower evaporates like mist in the sun. My body hums with desire, and my cock hardens to painful proportions. It's hunger and lust and desire all rolled into one, tempered with something deeper, something profound, something that feels very much like... love.

Her scent fills my nose as I hold her close, her breasts pressed against my chest. I cup her cheek, tilting her face to mine so I can drink her in. Her chestnut hair frames her pretty face and flushed cheeks. The freckles scattered across her nose are fucking adorable, and I want to kiss each one. My eyes drop to her full lips, watching as they part with her heavy breaths.

Yeah, she wants me as much as I want her.

"So, what happens now?" I murmur, sliding my nose along hers and kissing the corner of her mouth.

Jess bites her lip briefly, then pulls away from me and stands. I look up at her questioningly. Is she leaving me?

My eyes widen as her hands go to her blouse, and she begins to free buttons from buttonholes. She shrugs out of it, and it pools on the floor at her feet. She toes off her boots before sliding her pants down her thick, pale thighs and stepping out of them. Goosebumps break out across her smooth skin as she stands before me in her underwear. Her tits are barely contained in the lacy cups of her bra. Her nipples press against the fabric, and my mouth waters with the need to taste them. Her panties have little Christmas trees all over them, and my mouth tugs up in a smile.

"Fuck, you take my breath away, Jess. You're fucking adorable," I growl, coming to stand in front of her. I cup her face in my hand. "Are you sure this is what you want? That *I'm* what you want?'

She nods, licking her lips nervously. "I've never felt this way about anyone, Connor. It's kind of scary."

"I feel it, too, sweetheart," I admit, my heart beating a military tattoo against my ribs.

Without thinking any further, I take her mouth in a fervent kiss, infusing it with every ounce of the passion burning inside me. Her tongue meets mine in a frenzy of need, and a low moan echoes up from her throat into my mouth. Jesus, she tastes like cinnamon and sin, and I want to savor every inch of her smooth flesh.

I break the kiss and look down at Jess, noting her swollen lips and the splash of color across her cheeks. She's breathing hard, and her eyes are hooded with desire.

"You're so fucking beautiful," I mutter, skimming my hands down her shoulders and across the swell of her breasts.

Reaching behind her, I unclip her bra, smoothing the straps down her arms. Holy fucking shit, she has the most perfect breasts I've ever seen. Large and round and crowned with rosy nipples that harden as I watch. I want to throw her down on the blankets and rut into her like a wild animal. I swallow hard, fighting to get myself under control.

I wrap one arm around her waist while the other goes to the waistband of her panties. "Can I touch you, Jess?"

"Please," she gasps, moving her hips against me.

I slip my hand inside, encountering soft curls. My cock pulses in my pants as I feel the wetness that coats her pussy. Sliding a finger along her slit, I open her up to find her little nub.

"Oh, fuck, that feels good!" she gasps, jerking against me as my finger rubs over the target.

I watch her the whole time as I move my hand on her, her pleasure feeding mine as her head falls back and she calls my name. Her thighs tremble against mine. She needs to lie down before her legs give way.

I nudge her backward so she sinks onto the blanket-covered cushions, naked apart from the scrap of material covering her pussy. Her hair fans out around her, and my heart clenches at the sight. She's like Aphrodite, all luscious curves and creamy skin.

Jess's eyes stay glued to me as I rip my shirt over my head and kick off my boots. I unzip my pants and remove them, along with my boxers. My cock stands proudly to attention, angling up toward my stomach.

"You're so handsome. And so big," Jess whispers, her eyes on my turgid cock.

"You're good for my ego," I smile, kneeling in front of her and ripping her panties down her thighs. I bring them to my nose and inhale the damp spot from her juices before tossing them to one side.

"I want to taste you, Jess. Wanna put my mouth on you and feel you come on my tongue," I mutter, my eyes fixed on her glistening pussy.

"Oh, God, yes!" she says huskily, lifting her hips in a mute invitation.

I wrap my hand around her calf and lift her leg over my shoulder. "Jesus, you're wet for me, baby. So soft and tempting."

I nibble a path up her inner thigh, licking and sucking at her flesh before repeating the same on the other side.

"Connor, please!" Jess pants, lifting her hips to get me where she needs me the most.

"Please, what, sweetheart?"

"P-please put your m-mouth on me," she pleads.

I dive in, burying my whole face in her pussy and swirling my tongue around her clit.

"Connor!"

My hands bite into her squirming hips to hold her steady while I eat her out noisily, using my mouth, tongue, and teeth to drive her crazy. I circle her clit with my tongue before spearing the tip into her tight hole. She moans and jerks above me as I slip one, then another finger inside her, using her juices as lubrication as I thrust them in and out, fucking her with them.

Jess's head thrashes as I hook my fingers around, seeking out the sweet spot inside her, wanting to give her pleasure unlike anything she's ever experienced before.

"Oh! Oh! I—Connor!"

Jess shouts my name as she goes over the edge. Her body spasms and her pussy locks down on my fingers as her orgasm rips through her. I don't let up. I press my thumb against her clit and continue to thrust my fingers in and out of her tight entrance, extending her orgasm.

Finally, she falls limp, her chest rising and falling with her harsh breaths. I crawl up her body, scattering kisses along the way before sucking a hard nipple into my mouth.

"Connor," she sighs, meeting the thrust of my tongue as I claim her mouth in a desperate kiss.

"That is the sexiest fucking thing I've ever witnessed," I rasp, biting down gently on her bottom lip.

"I've never... no one has ever..." she trails off, her hazel eyes still heavy with the remnants of her pleasure.

"Am I the first man to put my mouth on you like that, Jess?"

"Yes," she whispers, her cheeks on fire.

I smooth her hair away from her flushed cheeks. "I'm honored. And I aim to please," I add with a grin.

"Oh, you pleased, all right," she murmurs, tilting her head back, greedy for more of my kisses.

My hard cock nudges her stomach, and she reaches between us, wrapping her hand around me. My breath hisses out as she gives me a squeeze, moving her hand up and down my length.

"Like this?" she asks, her eyes seeking mine for guidance.

"A little tighter, baby," I grunt, thrusting helplessly into her hand. "Yeah, like that. Fuck!" My jaw clenches, and I swallow hard as she slides her thumb across the end, swirling a bead of pre-cum around the slit. "Need inside you, Jess. So fucking bad!"

"God, yes, I want that too!" she moans, guiding my cock through her slick folds and notching me at her entrance. "Make love to me, Connor."

My breath rasps in my throat as she moves her hips

back and forth on my length, crying out as the head of my cock bumps her clit.

"You want my cock inside you, sweetheart?" I whisper against her lips.

"Yes!" she says immediately.

I link my hands with hers, pinning them above her head. I flex my hips, pushing inside her tight warmth just an inch. Then I stop.

"Fuck!"

"What is it? What's wrong?" Jess asks worriedly.

I force myself to hold still, eight inches from paradise. "I don't have any protection."

Jessica blinks. Then bites her lip. "I'm on the pill."

"I'm clean, baby. Haven't been with anyone for, Christ, for about ten fucking years," I admit, feeling embarrassed color hit my cheeks.

Jess's eyes widen in shock.

"You're it for me. I love you, Jess," I whisper against her soft lips. "I didn't know falling in love could happen so fucking fast. But I think it happened the first time you walked into my office with a mug of coffee and that big smile. The one that lights up the whole fucking building."

Her beautiful eyes meet mine, her lashes wet with her tears. "I love you, too, Connor. Have done since I first clapped eyes on your manly chest and bulging biceps."

I burst out laughing. "God, you're precious! I've never met anyone like you."

"Then it's about time you made me yours, Connor," she whispers, a tear rolling from the corner of her eye.

I kiss it away. I intend to spend the rest of my life kissing her tears away, only I hope any future tears will be happy ones.

I claim her mouth in a kiss, trying to convey the depth of my emotions as I slide inside her with one firm thrust. "Jesus, baby. You're so fucking tight," I grunt, forcing myself to hold still.

"Give me a second. You're big," she chokes, pressing her forehead against mine and tightening her fingers around mine.

"Just breathe, baby," I whisper, sliding my nose along her and feathering kisses all over her face. "You feel amazing, Jess. I'm never letting you go, you hear me? You're mine, and I'm yours."

"That's good because I'm never giving you back," she vows, her eyes shiny with emotion. She moves beneath me experimentally, and we both groan. "Feels...amazing. Please, move, Connor!"

I tilt my hips forward, sinking into her even more deeply. She moans, and I release her hands to plant mine beside her and brace my weight. We're made to fit together. She squeezes me so perfectly, warm and wet and tight.

Jess presses her head back into the blankets as I surge into her, picking up my pace. I hook a hand under her knee and lift her leg around my waist so I can go deeper, bottoming out inside her.

"God, so good...so good!" I grunt, pounding into her now.

This is our first time together. I should be taking it easy, drawing it out, but when she cries out and grabs my ass to pull me closer, any semblance of control I had shatters.

I look down as our bodies come together, hardness disappearing into softness. Sexiest goddamn thing I've ever seen, apart from watching her come on my mouth earlier. My balls slap her ass, and her large breasts shake and jiggle as I pummel her.

"God, look at you," I say in awe, my eyes skimming over her soft belly and wide hips. "Fucking perfect. And all mine."

Her walls tighten around my cock at my words, and I drop my head, pulling a nipple into my mouth.

"Connor! God...don't stop, please. I'm going to . . ."

"Give it to me, baby. Let go and come all over my cock," I command.

She sobs as her orgasm takes her, and she wails her release, face scrunched up, body jerking against me. With one last thrust, I follow her into heaven, shooting rope after rope of sticky cum into her welcoming cunt. On and on it goes, holding me rigid above her. I'm not only releasing my seed but also my grief and trauma, emptying it into her in cathartic waves that leave me sated and peaceful.

"Jess," I choke, collapsing on top of her.

"I've got you," she whispers. "I love you."

I'm surprised to discover my eyes are wet. I haven't cried since I was a boy. Jessica scatters kisses across my face, wrapping her whole body around me, giving me a kind of comfort I didn't know I needed until now.

"I love you," I mutter, seeking out her lips for a tender kiss.

Her love gives me strength, and just like that, I let it all go. For the first time since the incident, I feel like I can truly move forward with the angel in my arms.

Chapter 7
Jessica

Once the storm unleashes its heavy load outside, one night becomes two, secluding us in our private little world. We eat junk food and laugh and talk for hours. I find myself sharing things with Connor I've never shared with anyone else. How devastated I was when my dad died from cancer when I was seven. How my mom couldn't cope and took off with another man, leaving my grandma to raise me.

Sadly, Connor also lost his dad at an early age, a tragic coincidence that deepens our bond. He talks about his sister, Rosie, and it's clear how much he loves her. Seeing his love for his family makes me fall in love with him a little more.

We dig out the office Christmas tree and decorate it with the box in the staff room. We also stumble across some board games and a deck of cards, and while away the hours playing and laughing and talking.

By some miracle, there aren't any major incidents. Drayton calls early the first morning, asking if I can look up a phone number for Chloe Jenkins. She threw her daughter, Daisy, out of the house in the storm. Luckily, Drayton was on hand to rescue Daisy from her car before she froze to death but knew Daisy would want to check on her mom—who was hungover but fine.

Daisy is a sweetheart and took over the barmaid job at The Hideaway to help keep a roof over her mom's head. It's the worst-kept secret in town that Chloe Jenkins is an alcoholic. It's why Daisy returned to Garland a few months ago—a seemingly futile attempt to get her mother back on the straight and narrow.

"What time is it?" I ask, snuggling into Connor's warm body beneath the blankets. My makeshift picnic area has doubled as a makeshift bed for the last two nights.

"Almost six," Connor replies, smoothing his hands down my bare back.

"I guess we should get dressed," I sigh, reluctant to leave this little slice of heaven. The doubts are already starting to creep in. Will Connor still feel the same once we're back in the real world? Or will it be business as usual?

Connor tilts my chin so I'm looking at him. "I can see those cogs turning in your brain. What's up?"

My smile is a little wobbly. "Just wondering how this is going to work once we get back to reality," I say, waving a finger between us.

He frowns. "Because we work together?"

I nod. "That and . . . will you still want me, you know, in the cold light of day, so to speak?"

Connor's mouth tightens in what I've already come to recognize as suppressed frustration. "Sweetheart, I thought I made my feelings clear over the last few days. Every time I kissed you. Every time I touched you. Every time I buried myself inside you and watched you come. Jess, these last two days have been everything because you're everything."

"Ah, crap. Now you've made me cry again," I sniff, wiping away the tears that trickle down my cheeks. "I love you, Connor. So much."

He kisses me tenderly. "I love you, too, baby."

I wrap my arms around him, allowing his words to sink in and heal some of the damage inflicted by my ex. Connor's right. So long as there's love, we can face anything.

Four hours later, the pathways around the station have been cleared. The snowplows have cleared the roads, and things are beginning to get back to normal after the storm.

Connor and I make it to mid-morning before he manhandles me into the small staff room and backs me up against the wall, kissing me as if he hasn't seen me for weeks.

Sadly, our interlude is short-lived as the door opens, and we jump apart guiltily. Drayton comes to an abrupt halt, and his gaze moves between the two of us suspiciously.

"Oh! Hey, boss," Connor says casually, turning away to hide his obvious erection.

"I—It's not what it seems like," I stutter, nervousness biting at my insides. "I, uh, had something in my eye, and Connor was checking it for me."

I had something in my eye? Really?

"Didn't realize an eye examination involved both of your tongues. And I sure as hell hope it is what it looks like because you two have been dancing around each other for months," Drayton says, his mouth twitching with a suppressed smile.

I open my mouth to reply, but Drayton continues.

"When Connor has finished checking your eye, perhaps you could look over the report I'm about to email you."

I nod my head so fast that I almost give myself whiplash. Cheeks burning, I leave the room and make a beeline for my desk.

One week slips past, and then another. My feet barely touch the ground. When I'm not working, I'm with Connor at my tiny apartment above the bakery in town or his place. He lives in a converted barn on the edge of town that still needs some work, but I adore it. I wander through the rooms, adding feminine touches in my head and getting dreamy-eyed as I picture a nursery filled with baby stuff.

Every day we grow closer, to the point where I can't remember a time when we weren't together. It's hell keeping our hands off each other during our working day while we try to remain professional. Once we get home, we often don't make it to the bedroom before he's inside me, wringing me out with a toe-curling orgasm. He constantly tells me how much he loves my body, my curves, how much I turn him on, and how I'm the sexiest woman he's ever known.

But I should've known that life would throw us a shitty curveball in the shape of a phone call late one night when Connor is staying at my apartment. I wake, groggy-eyed, to hear him answer the call.

"*What?* When? Is she . . . will she be okay?"

The urgency and fear in his voice suddenly have me wide awake.

"Fuck! I'll get the next flight. Be there as soon as I can." He ends the call and turns to look at me, his expression tortured. "That was my mom. There was a fire at Rosie's apartment block. Rosie was inside. She's been taken to the hospital."

My hand flies to my mouth in shock. "Oh, my God! I'm so sorry, Connor!"

"I have to go," he says, standing and quickly pulling on his clothes.

"I'll come with you," I say immediately, reaching for my clothes.

Connor sits on the edge of the bed and hauls me into his arms. "No, baby. It's better if you stay here. Apart from anything else, Drayton won't cope with both of us gone."

I nod, knowing he's right. "Okay. I'll take care of everything here. You just get to Rosie. She's your priority right now."

Connor drops his forehead to mine. "You're amazing, you know that?"

"I'm beginning to because of you," I reply, summoning a smile. "Now go. And call me."

He kisses me quick and hard. I watch as he walks out the door, taking a piece of my heart with him.

Connor calls me as soon as he gets to the hospital in Houston to fill me in on Rosie's condition. She's suffered burns to her neck and back and is being treated for smoke inhalation. She may be left with some permanent scarring from the burns, but the doctors are optimistic that there will be no lasting damage to her lungs from the smoke inhalation. My heart breaks for her, even though we've never met, and I can only imagine what Connor and the rest of his family are going through.

Connor tells me he plans to stay in Houston a little longer to be nearby if needed.

I bury myself in work, and one week becomes two. I miss Connor like crazy. He calls daily to update me, but not seeing or touching him is agony. I'm desperate to join him in Houston, but work is hectic, and my conscience won't allow me to leave Drayton in the lurch while his deputy is also on compassionate leave. Anyway, I'm being selfish. It's a few weeks out of the rest of our lives together—because I know that's what I want—to live out the rest of my days with the man I love more than anything else in the whole world. He's my everything—loving, generous, strong, and sexy as hell.

Christmas is fast approaching, so I dig out my small tree and decorations one evening after work. I string up some fairy lights and put out my favorite sparkly Christmas candles—the ones I never light because they're too pretty. When I'm done, I stand back to admire my handiwork.

"What do you think, Dave?" I ask the tabby curled up on the sofa. He opens one eye, totally unimpressed, and immediately goes back to sleep.

"Well, I think it looks cozy and festive. I think I'll bake some Christmas cookies even though the big day is still a week away," I tell my uninterested companion.

Thirty minutes later, the smell of gingerbread and cinnamon fills my tiny apartment and lifts my spirits. I've always loved Christmas and was hoping to share it with Connor this year, but he'll still be in Houston the way things are looking.

Once the cookies are done, I spend the evening watching re-runs of 'Friends' before heading to bed. I miss the warmth of Connor's body next to me. I miss his touch, his kiss, and the sense of belonging he invokes within me.

A few more days slip past, and before I know it, it's the day before Christmas Eve. I'm sitting at my desk just after lunch with my head buried in a report about a break-in at the local library when Drayton calls me into his office.

"Hey, boss. What do you need?" I ask, looking at the sheriff as he sits behind his desk.

He's a big guy and intimidating if you don't know him. Thank God he's one of the good guys.

"Take a seat, Jess," he says somberly, indicating the chair opposite him.

"Oh, shit! What's up?" I ask, my heart thumping in my chest at his serious expression.

Drayton leans back in his chair. "I appreciate that you and Connor have tried to keep things professional at work, but—"

"You're not going to fire me, are you? Or Connor?" I cut across him. "I mean, I know it kind of muddies the waters, what with us being in a relationship and working together and all, but I don't think there's anything written anywhere that says we can't be together, and you know I'd never let our relationship distract me from doing my job properly, so—"

I grind to a halt as Drayton holds up a big hand, his mouth twitching with a smile behind his beard.

"No, I'm not going to fire you or Connor, Jess. I was going to say that I appreciate you trying to keep things professional at work, but you don't need to hide the fact that you're in a relationship. It's currently the worst-kept secret in the station, and the fact that you've been walking around like a lost puppy for the last few weeks proves how you feel about him."

I grimace. "I thought I was hiding it well, but I miss him like crazy. Don't get me wrong. I'm glad he's there for his sister, but—" I stop, embarrassed to suddenly find myself fighting back the tears.

"But it's tough being away from someone you love," Drayton finishes, leaning across the desk to hand me a tissue.

"Yeah," I whisper, dabbing at my eyes. I look up at him. "So, you and Daisy Jenkins, huh?"

Drayton's cheeks turn ruddy.

"Sorry, I didn't mean to embarrass you. Sometimes, my mouth engages before my brain can intervene," I say wryly,

"It's fine," he assures me. "And yes, Daisy and I are together."

"I've met her a few times at The Hideout. She's a wonderful person," I say.

"That she is," Drayton agrees, his eyes softening. He clears his throat. "Anyway, that's not why I called you in here. I don't suppose you have a key to Connor's place?"

My eyebrows rise in surprise. That's the last thing I expected him to ask. "Uh, yeah, I do. Why?"

"Because he took a file home with him to work on before he left for Houston that I need. I wondered if you could go get it for me?"

I nod. "Sure. I'll go now if you don't need me for the next hour or so?"

"Great. I'll see you in a bit."

Snow still blankets everything, and there are piles of it on the sides of the roads where the snowplows cleared it after the storm. Although we haven't had any more snowfall, the temperatures are still below freezing most days, making for icy conditions, which are more of a problem than the snow.

Twenty minutes later, I pull up outside Connor's place. I park my little VW on his drive and walk up the path toward the front door. I let myself in and head straight for the first door on the left that leads into his study. Spotting the file on the desk, I grab it and turn to leave when soft music reaches my ears.

Is that *Let It Snow* by Dean Martin I can hear? I shake my head. Probably one of the neighbors getting in the Christmas spirit. Then I remember there *are* no neighbors.

I follow the sound of the music toward the living area at the back of the house. Lights flicker up ahead, twinkling on and off. I step on something with my booted foot and see rose petals scattered across the floor in a floral trail, leading me closer to the living area.

What the…?

My heart is beating in my throat, and my mouth is dry. Has someone broken in? Should I call Drayton? Why would they put up Christmas lights and scatter rose petals all over the floor?

Unless…

I poke my head through the doorway, and my heart stops completely. The file slips from my hand and lands on the floor with a thud.

"Connor?"

He's wearing a suit, complete with a crisp white shirt and a bowtie. He's holding a bouquet of roses, a lopsided grin on his handsome face. He's the most beautiful sight I've ever seen.

"Connor!" I'll probably be embarrassed later by my ridiculously girly squeal, but right now, I don't give a crap.

I sprint toward him with the grace of a three-legged reindeer and launch myself into his arms, crushing the flowers between us. He catches me with a deep chuckle, and I grab his face, scattering kisses over every inch of skin I can reach.

"You're back!" I beam at him, running my hands all over his face to make sure I'm not dreaming.

"Did you miss me?" he asks, his striking blue eyes twinkling with mirth.

"Like a squirrel misses his nuts," I nod enthusiastically. "When did you get back? How is Rosie? Why didn't you call me?"

Connor laughs and hugs me close. "Two hours ago. Rosie is doing fine. And I wanted to surprise you," he says, answering my questions in order. "Because . . ."

He steps back and drops to one knee, pulling a small velvet box from his pocket and opening it.

I stagger back with a gasp at the sight of the engagement ring sitting inside the small box. I cover my gaping mouth and stare at him with wide eyes.

Connor looks up at me, and the raw emotion in his eyes robs me of breath and turns my inside to goo. "I love you with all my heart. Being away from you for the last few weeks has been torture. I don't ever want us to be apart again. Will you marry me, Jess?"

Tears well and spill over, and all I can do is nod. Connor stands and slips the ring onto my finger before pulling me in for a blistering kiss that has my toes curling up in my boots. We're both disheveled and breathing heavily when he finally lets me up for air. I let out another embarrassing squeal as he swings me up in his arms.

"What are you doing?" I laugh, wrapping my arms around his neck.

"Taking my fiancée to bed so I can show her how much I love her, how much I've missed her," he mutters, dropping a quick kiss on my mouth.

"But I have to get back to work. Drayton needs the file I dropped on the living room floor."

Connor grins. "No, he doesn't."

I narrow my eyes at him suspiciously. "Oh?"

"Drayton isn't expecting us back at work until after Christmas," he explains.

The penny drops. "Drayton knew you were planning to propose?"

Connor nods. "I called him yesterday to tell him I was on my way back and ask him for a favor. He was only too happy to help, seeing as he's planning a proposal of his own."

"He's going to ask Daisy to marry him?" I ask excitedly, and Connor nods again. "He never mentioned a thing earlier. My God, you men, and your evil plotting."

Connor leers at me as he tosses me onto his large bed. "Plotting my way into your panties, baby. What

Christmas delight are you wearing today?" he asks, tugging off my boots and yanking my pants down my legs. "Gingerbread men, huh? You trying to make me jealous?"

I snort with laughter. "Calm down, honey. They're not real men."

Connor growls as he hooks his thumbs into the waistband and rips them from my body. He brings them to his nose, inhaling deeply.

"Holy shit, that was hot," I pant, my body immediately on fire for him.

"God, I've missed you, baby. Missed this gorgeous body," he mutters, his eyes on my glistening pussy. "But most of all, I've missed your beautiful smile and how you make me feel. I've never met anyone like you, Jess. You give me a sense of peace and belonging I've never had before."

"I missed you so much, it hurt," I whisper through a throat thick with tears.

"I'm back now, baby. And the next time we go anywhere, it'll be together."

"Good," I nod. "Now, please get your clothes off and get inside me. I need you!"

Connor doesn't need to be asked twice. Our clothes come off in record time, and then he's lowering himself on top of me, skin to skin, heart to heart. His fingers immediately find my pussy, opening me up to the sheer magic of his touch.

"Jesus, sweetheart. You're so wet for me," he grunts, flicking his finger across my clit.

I cry out, desperate to have him inside me. Reaching between us, I grab his cock and guide him to my entrance. "Please, Connor! I need you so badly. I want you to fuck me hard."

My words seem to unleash a primitive part of him, and he surges inside me with one powerful thrust. He always stretches me to a point just shy of pain, and we both cry out as he seats himself deep inside me. He's home. Right where he belongs.

He flips us over, so I'm straddling him, giving control over to me. I ride him like a woman possessed, fucking myself on his thick cock.

"Goddamn, woman. Look at you!" he grunts, watching my breasts bounce up and down as I move on him. "Fucking gorgeous."

He keeps talking to me, telling me how amazing I am, how lucky he is, and that I'm his everything. It only takes seconds before my orgasm slams into me, and I scream my release as my pussy locks down on him.

Connor is right behind me, shouting as he tumbles over the edge and shoots me full of his sticky cum.

"Fuck . . . oh, fuck, Jess!" he grunts, his hands clamping down on my hips as he empties himself inside me.

I collapse onto his chest, sweaty and breathless, wriggling my hips as little aftershocks pulse through me.

"You're mine," I whisper against his chest.

"Always, sweetheart."

I smile against his chest and fall into a blissful sleep. In two days, it will be Christmas. The best one ever.

Epilogue
Jessica

One Year Later

You'd think I'd be used to it by now—the way he looks at me like he wants to devour me. But nope. One year together, and I still short-circuit every time my husband walks into a room and sets his blue-eyed, panty-melting gaze on me like I'm the prize in a Christmas cracker he never thought he'd win.

"You're staring again," I say, glancing up from the mixing bowl and trying not to blush like it's our first date and not the third time this week I've baked in nothing but his oversized T-shirt and fuzzy reindeer socks.

Connor leans against the doorframe, arms folded over that unfairly delicious chest, a lazy smile on his lips. "Can't help it. My girl's baking Christmas cookies in my shirt, looking like the centerfold of a holiday pin-up calendar.”

“You say that like I didn't just get flour in my cleavage,” I deadpan, swiping at the puff of white dust now coating my chest.

His smile widens. “Still the best place for it.”

He crosses the kitchen in three strides and slides his arms around me from behind, pressing a warm kiss to the crook of my neck. I shiver. Like always. This man could make me combust just by breathing near me.

“Mmm. You smell like gingerbread and temptation,” he murmurs, voice thick with heat.

“Careful, Deputy. That kind of talk'll get you extra cookies. And a spanking.”

Connor growls low in his throat, nipping gently at my earlobe. “Is that a promise?”

The oven dings before I can reply, and I wiggle out of his arms because—priorities. “Cookies now. Kinks later.”

He laughs, and God, that laugh still wrecks me. Deep and warm and safe.

I pull the tray from the oven and slide the golden, sugar-dusted stars onto the cooling rack. “So. Remind me what we've got tonight?”

Connor hands me a fresh mug of peppermint cocoa like the domestic god he is. "Tree lighting in the town square at six. Caroling after. You promised to judge the gingerbread contest. And then we're hosting game night at the station."

"Oh, right. That's not a packed schedule at all," I say, sipping the cocoa. "I might need a nap between the tinsel and the trivia."

He leans in and kisses my nose. "Already scheduled it into the calendar. Hot sex followed by mandatory snuggling."

I melt. Like one of those cartoon characters whose heart puffs out of their chest in pink bubbles.

It's surreal, sometimes, how much can change in a year. Last Christmas, we were snowed in, dancing around our feelings like nervous reindeer on a slippery roof. Now we're living together in Connor's renovated barn, waking up tangled in flannel sheets and fuzzy cats, building a life that feels equal parts cozy and chaotic.

Dave the Cat even tolerates Connor now. Well. Mostly. He still tries to steal his bacon in the mornings, but I count that as a win.

Connor watches me from across the kitchen as I layer more cookie dough onto the tray, and I can tell he's about to say something serious by the soft crease between his brows.

"I got something for you," he says, sliding a small box from his jacket pocket.

"Connor, I told you we're not exchanging gifts until Christmas Eve," I say, already suspicious—and not-so-secretly delighted.

"It's not for Christmas." His voice is rougher now. "It's for now."

He crosses to me again and opens the box.

Inside is a delicate silver charm bracelet. Dangling from the chain are tiny, intricate charms: a snowflake, a star, a coffee mug, a badge, a gingerbread cookie, and a cat that looks suspiciously like Dave. My throat tightens.

"Each one is a piece of our story," he says. "The snowstorm. The night you brought me coffee and stole my heart. Those gingerbread panties almost killed me from lust. And that grumpy little menace who claws my boots and sleeps on my side of the bed."

I laugh, blinking fast to clear the tears from my eyes. "Connor..."

He lifts my hand and clasps the bracelet onto my wrist. "Next year, I'll add more charms. And the year after that. Every Christmas, I want to remember what we've built together. I want to mark every little memory. With you."

"I'm gonna cry," I warn, voice cracking.

"Good," he says gruffly. "Means I did it right."

I throw my arms around him, breathing him in. Cinnamon and cedar and that spicy cologne he only wears when I've been "good." Or, more accurately, when he plans to make me very, *very* bad.

"I love you," I whisper.

"Forever," he replies.

* * *

That night, we bundle up in scarves and coats and brave the snowy town square, where twinkling lights spiral up the lampposts and the scent of roasted chestnuts and mulled cider fills the air. Mayor Graham gives his annual speech, which is mostly him telling bad jokes and flirting with his long-suffering wife before hitting the big red button.

Lights blaze to life across the square, and the towering Christmas tree glitters like magic incarnate. Children squeal. Parents cheer. I lean into Connor's side, and he tucks his arm around me like I belong there. Which I do.

The gingerbread contest is predictably chaotic. Someone enters a gingerbread version of the sheriff's office, complete with cookie versions of the staff. Connor pretends not to be emotional, but I catch him snapping a photo with his phone when no one's looking.

Later, we walk hand-in-hand through the quiet streets back to the station, where Drayton and Daisy are already waiting with hot cider and a suspicious twinkle in their eyes.

"You two look disgustingly happy," he says, sipping from his mug.

Connor smirks. "Guess love does that to you."

"I think we've infected Officer Shaw and Ellie, the woman who delivers the sandwiches," I add, tipping my head in their direction to where they're snuggled up in the corner.

Drayton grins, his gaze soft as it flicks to Daisy. "Guess love has a way of finding those who need it most— present company included."

Daisy nudges him with her elbow, eyes twinkling. "You big softie."

He kisses the top of her head. "Only for you, sweetheart."

As game night winds down and I snuggle into Connor's lap with a blanket around my shoulders and his arms wrapped tight around me, I realize this... this is it. The life I never thought I deserved. The man I never thought would choose me. The love that came wrapped in flannel and snowstorms and a badge.

Claiming Christmas

Turns out, Christmas miracles aren't just for movies.

Sometimes, they show up at your desk, ask you about tire chains, and change your life forever.

81

Bonus Scene
Connor

Three Years Later

"Wake up, Daddy. It's Christmas Day," my wife says, rousing me from my slumber.

I groan and roll over, coming face to face with my two-year-old daughter, Lanie.

"Dada," she says, giving me a toothy grin.

"Hey, angel," I smile, dropping a kiss on her chestnut curls as she cuddles in next to me.

"Time to get up, sleepyhead. Santa's been," my wife says excitedly, moving into my line of vision as she lays down next to us.

"Mama," Lanie giggles and pats her mama's face with a chubby hand, her blue eyes dancing.

We were up until 2 AM wrapping presents and getting everything prepared for when my family arrives later. Rosie and her husband, Dex, with their little boy, and my mom and stepfather are all coming here for Christmas Day. They flew in the day before yesterday and are staying in a hotel in the next town. We would've had them stay here, but we're having some renovations to extend our home, making it impossible for us to accommodate guests.

"Come on!" Jess urges, bouncing up and down on the bed and making Lanie giggle again. Anyone would think Jess was the child, excited at the prospect of opening all her presents from Santa Claus.

I scoop up my daughter, blow a raspberry on her neck that makes her shriek with laughter, and hop out of bed. Jess quickly follows, and we head downstairs into the living room, where a giant Christmas tree stands in the corner. The smell of pine hits my nose, and I inhale deeply, absorbing the aroma of Christmas itself.

Jess has done a fantastic job decorating the house, although I'm pretty sure her remit was, if it doesn't move, decorate it. There are twinkling fairy lights, tinsel, baubles, snowflakes, and banners everywhere. I'm not complaining. I'd let my wife hang tinsel off my cock if it made her happy.

I put Lanie down, and she waddles towards the giant tree to investigate the presents beneath it, clapping her little hands happily. We haven't gone mad. Much as we love our daughter, we don't want to spoil her. At two years old, she doesn't yet understand all the fuss, but we want her to grow up knowing the true meaning of Christmas, not the commercial madness that seems to overshadow the most important element—family. So, we agreed on a budget for gifts and donated half to a local charity for homeless children so they, too, would have gifts to open today.

The last three years with Jess have been the happiest years of my life. It's hard to believe now that we danced around each other for months at work before a snowstorm finally forced us to admit our feelings for each other. Those two nights together at the station contain some of my most precious memories—along with our wedding day and the day Lanie was born. Hell, every fucking day with my beautiful wife and daughter is more precious than any gift beneath the tree.

Jess plucks a small silver-wrapped box from beneath the tree as I sink onto the floor next to Lanie. "Can you give that to Daddy, sweet pea?" she asks, handing the small package to our daughter.

Lanie turns to face me. "For Dada," she says, giving me the sweetest smile.

I look up at Jess in confusion. "I thought we said we weren't buying gifts for each other."

Jess shrugs. "It's only a little something."

I tear the paper off the package and open the box to reveal...

"A pregnancy test?" My eyes snap to Jess's. "You're pregnant?"

She grins and nods. "Like I said, it's only a little something. About the size of a pea right now."

I stand and wrap her up in my arms, kissing her fiercely. "Just when I thought I couldn't be any happier, you go and prove me wrong."

"It just keeps getting better and better, doesn't it?" she murmurs, her hazel eyes adoring on my face.

I claim her mouth in another kiss, tender and sweet. No words can express how much I love this woman in my arms. "The best is yet to come, baby. The best is yet to come."

Thank you for reading!

Reviews help readers discover new books! If you enjoyed **Claiming Christmas**, I'd love to hear what you enjoyed most—your review means the world to me and guides other readers to discover my work.

Love,

Violet x0x0

Continue reading for a sneak peek of Claiming Valentine.

Claiming Valentine
Sneak Peek

Link

I visit Valentine's Kitchen every day, trying to work up the courage to ask Natasha Valentine on a date. Delicious as her bakery's treats are, they don't compare to her sweet curves, ebony hair, and deep-brown eyes. I'm hooked from the first day.

When our first date ends disastrously, I'm left wondering where I went wrong. Walking away from her isn't an option because Tasha is unlike any woman I've ever known. I'm drawn to her in ways that go deeper than physical attraction.

Tasha thinks her Asperger's is a problem to keep us apart. I see it as a gift, an opportunity to connect, communicate, and understand each other better than many couples have the chance to do. I'll do whatever it takes to be the man she deserves and earn my place at her side for the rest of our lives.

Author's Note:

Claiming Valentine features a main character with Asperger's Syndrome. Asperger's Syndrome is a form of Autism Spectrum Syndrome, a neurobiological disorder where people have difficulty relating to others socially. Their behavior and thinking patterns can be rigid and repetitive.

Raising awareness of autism is a cause close to my heart as my son is on the autistic spectrum. Each person experiences autism differently, but it's important to know that it's not a "disease," and it's not something that needs to be "cured," but rather needs to be understood and embraced.

Claiming Valentine is a work of fiction and aims to highlight some of the struggles faced by people on the spectrum through Tasha and Link's love story.

Sneak Peek

Tash

Mornings are my favorite time of the day. It's just me in the kitchen with all my ingredients. I make sure to get them ready the night before, so all I need to do is take them out and put them in the order I'm going to use them.

I unlock the door of Valentine's Kitchen at 4 AM, as I do every morning except Sundays. It's not like I have far to go, living in the apartment above the bakery. The sun isn't even up yet, and the streets are so peaceful. There are no people around, which suits me fine—I'll have plenty of customers to deal with later once the doors open.

I inhale deeply as I enter the shop. The kitchen still smells delicious from all the baked goods yesterday, and the aroma is comforting. I slip automatically into my morning routine, starting with preparing my coffee. I have a special brew I like to make up just for me. The beans are in the fridge, and I take pleasure in the sound of them grinding. The smell they release is pure heaven.

There are a lot of sounds and smells I can't tolerate, but the sound and smell of grinding coffee beans isn't one of them.

While the coffee brews, I get my kitchen set up how I like it.

I know I could come in later and still finish all my work for the day. I wouldn't have to go to bed so early. But being alone in my kitchen, doing things my way, and not worrying about someone moving something when I'm not looking is my idea of heaven.

By the time the coffee is done brewing and my counter-tops are set up with all the ingredients I plan to use for baking, the sun is starting to come up.

I like that there aren't any cars on the streets yet. The only sound is the birds waking up. I stand at the back door, letting the cool breeze caress my skin as I talk to the birds.

"Good morning, tweeters," I croon, watching them swoop and land, wings twitching and heads bobbing as they peck at the cake crumbs I've tossed on the ground

I've called birds tweeters ever since I was a child. My mom likes to tell the story about how I would kneel on the couch at the window, chattering in my baby talk. The only thing she could understand was the word "tweeters." I'm not sure where I came up with that. Even now, as an adult, I can't seem to make the switch to calling them birds, like every other adult on the face of the earth. I've stopped trying. So long as *I* know what I mean, does it matter?

"I'm making some jam tarts today and, of course, fresh bread. What are you doing? Building nests? I'll bring you some more treats later."

It's never occurred to me that talking to birds might be strange. On some level, I know people might think so, but I'm beyond the point of trying to be "normal"—whatever that means. Just more boxes to tick and try to fit into.

I head back inside just as Alexa, my regular day staff, arrives. I'm fortunate I don't need more than one employee at a time because I can't deal with too many people around me.

Alexa opens up the bakery for the day and serves the customers out front while I immerse myself in baking out back in the kitchen.

As I work, my focus is interrupted for the briefest moment. A masculine face slides into my mind, and I shake my head to get rid of it. I don't like being interrupted when I'm baking—even if it is my random thoughts about a certain handsome guy with bright blue eyes who comes in every day.

"Tasha, can I leave early today?" Alexa asks, appearing behind me a couple of hours later as I mix up the batter for the muffins.

At eighteen, Alexa is unpredictable and impulsive at times. Although, I shouldn't blame her age. Unpredictability and impulsiveness are foreign concepts to me. My life is one of structure and routine.

The idea of breaking our daily schedule makes me anxious. "Is it necessary?"

"I'm sorry, but yes, it is. I've had a horrible toothache for days, and I've been taking a shit ton, uh, I mean, a lot of painkillers, but they're not helping. The dentist just called to say there's a cancellation," Alexa explains with what I think is a pleading expression. "I said I'd take it. I need to be there by 2 PM."

I take a deep breath, reminding myself that this isn't a big deal. It's usually quiet after that time, and I can easily manage myself. I'll only need to cover on my own until 4 PM when Lisa comes in.

I nod my head. "I understand. Of course, you should go and take care of that."

"Thanks, Tasha," Alexa replies gratefully.

I nod. "No problem."

Alexa returns to the counter, and I take a break to call my best friend, Belle. She and I trained together at Molly Black's culinary school in Medicine Bow. Her training was interrupted by her mother's death, and her grandmother came to take her back to Jasper and the ranch where she grew up. I need to check in with her and find out how she's doing.

"Hey, Tash," Belle greets me after the second ring.

"How are you?" I ask immediately.

"Ah, you know." Belle sighs down the line. "Actually, you don't, do you?" she asks, although the question is rhetorical.

Belle gets me better than anyone other than my parents. She's never made me feel awkward and never treated me any differently.

"Let's see," she continues. "I've just lost my mom, Grams is dying of cancer, and a month ago, I married a man I've been in love with for years to protect the ranch and my inheritance. So, yeah, I guess overwhelmed is one way of putting it," she says dryly.

I know all about feeling overwhelmed, although mine is more of a physical stimuli thing. "I'm sorry. That sucks. Want me to package up some of my chocolate cupcakes and mail them to you?" I ask, coming up with the only way I know how to cheer her up.

"That would be amazing. You know how much I love your cupcakes. Almost as much as I love your pastries."

"Ah, my croissants and pain au chocolat. I'll make some just for you," I promise.

"What would I do without you?"

"Not have cupcakes, croissants, or pain au chocolat."

Belle's soft laugh reaches me down the line. "True. So how are things in Garland? Is Valentine's Kitchen still pulling in the customers?"

Belle and I talk for a few more minutes before I need to get back to work. It's always good to hear my friend's voice, and we promise to call again in a few days.

The next couple of hours fly, and before I know it, Alexa is heading out the door for her dental appointment. Just after she leaves, the door chime jingles, and I look up with my professional smile firmly fixed on my face.

It's *him.* Link Thompson.

Steely blue eyes, strong nose, high cheekbones, and a body that makes me weak in the knees. I hate it when he comes in and makes me feel this way. So out of control. But I love it at the same time.

"Good morning, Tasha."

His deep voice makes my heart jump around. I could listen to him talk all day. If only he wanted to talk to me for that long.

"Good morning, Link." I give him what I think passes for a genuine smile. "What can I get for you today?"

"Well, that depends," he says, blue eyes twinkling. "What are you offering?"

"I made some jam tarts this morning. There's raspberry, strawberry, and blueberry," I reply, pointing them out in the display case.

"Those sound good. I'm sure the guys at the garage will love them. Can I get half a dozen? Two of each?"

I busy myself with putting them in a box.

"And three cups of that amazing coffee you make."

"One black, the other two are cream and sugar, right?"

Link shakes his head and laughs.

I frown. Did I say something funny?

"You have the best memory of anyone I've ever met,"

he says, and I think that's appreciation I see in his eyes as he looks at me.

I'm not vain, but I know the opposite sex finds me physically attractive. I'm not beautiful, but my long, black hair and abundance of curves seem to appeal to men—not that I've taken up the offer of a date with either of the men who've asked me since I moved here. They may like the packaging, but they have no idea how to deal with the woman beneath the pretty wrapping paper.

"I'm just good with details," I reply in response to Link's comment. "I know the black coffee is for you. I remember you telling me you don't like messing up your coffee with cream and sugar. And the other two are for Brett and Jim, who seem to have no problem destroying a perfectly good cup of coffee with both" I wrinkle my nose in distaste.

"I know, right?" Link agrees with a smile. "I keep threatening to set the coffee police on them."

I tilt my head as I look at him. "That's a real thing?"

Link's blond eyebrows rise. "The coffee police? No, but it should be," he replies with a wink, making my stomach flutter.

I finish putting the coffees in a tray and hand them to him along with the box of pastries before giving him the total.

Carefully, Link counts out the exact change. He always has exact change. I appreciate that. Most people these days use debit cards, but Link always seems to have cash.

"Thank you, Link."

He lingers for a moment, and I wonder if he's forgotten something. Or maybe I did. What did I forget?

"Are you going to the fishing derby this weekend?" he asks.

I can't stop myself from making a face. "No, I don't fish."

He laughs. "No. You don't strike me as someone who fishes."

I wonder what that means, but I don't know how to ask. Everyone around here fishes, and they seem to think it's fun. I don't get it. I feel bad for those poor fish. They get hooked and then thrown back into the lake like they're supposed to go about their lives after being teased by worms, only to end up on a hook. It must be so traumatic.

"What do you do for fun, Tasha?"

I wonder why he's asking me these questions, but I answer anyway. "I bake."

"That's your job. What do you do when you aren't baking?"

I don't understand the question. Baking is fun. "I, um, I eat what I bake. Or I sell it. Or sometimes, I take it to the shelter because I know they don't get sweet treats very often. I like watching people enjoy what I make."

He studies me thoughtfully. "That's generous of you. Do you eat stuff other than your baking?"

Such a silly question. "Of course."

"Would you like to eat stuff other than your baking with me sometime?" he asks.

The company would be nice. I think. I usually eat whatever is simple and easy at home with my cat, George.

I nod. "Sure."

"Great."

The smile on his face tells me I've given the right answer, and it sets off a spark inside me. I've made him happy. That makes me feel warm inside. It's not a feeling I'm overly familiar with.

"How about tonight?"

Tonight? I panic. My favorite show is on at 9 PM. That's later than my usual bedtime, but I come in a little later on Saturdays so I can stay up until 10 PM. Will I be home in time to watch my show?

"I guess I could do that. I have to be home by nine, though. You know I live in the apartment above the bakery, right?" I ask, pointing a finger toward the ceiling.

He grins. "Oh, believe me, I know."

He reaches out and touches my hand, and I pull back instinctively. The unexpected tactile contact takes me by surprise, and the warmth of his skin does odd things to my heart rate.

Link frowns. "I'm sure I can have you home by then, but only if you're sure you want to go."

"I do," I say, reassuring him—and myself.

I *do* want to eat with Link. I don't think he considers this a date or anything, but it would be nice to have him as a friend...

About the Author

Loved this book?

Find more steamy romances from Violet Rae:

www.authorvioletrae.com

Violet Rae writes spicy, emotionally charged romances where the connection is instant, the heroes are protective (and a little bit unhinged for their woman), and the heat level threatens to set off smoke alarms. From fated mates in outer space to small-town rescues and paranormal standoffs, Violet's stories deliver fast love, fierce devotion, and that delicious fantasy of being utterly cherished.

There's always a woman in danger (or simply in need of a serious nap), a hero who will burn down the world for her, and just enough humor to make you snort-laugh between kisses and kidnappings. Found families, caretaking intimacy, dirty talk, and happily-ever-afters are guaranteed—along with a little chaos, a lot of heart, and the kind of chemistry that makes your eReader blush.

Fast love. Fierce devotion. Delicious fantasies.

Violet is the original creator of the following multi author series':

Monster Between the Sheets

Dad Bod: Men Built for Comfort

Dad Bod: Large and in Charge

Dad Bod: Christmas

Dad Bod: Monster Edition

Filthy Fairy Tales

www.ingramcontent.com/pod-product-compliance
Lightning Source LLC
Chambersburg PA
CBHW051233160726
47994CB00002B/865